59446
Goats Don't Brush Their Teeth

Trina Wiebe
AR B.L.: 4.0
Points: 2.0

Goats Don't Brush Their Teeth

by Trina Wiebe

Illustrations
by Marisol Sarrazin

Lobster Press ™

*In memory of my grandmother, Antonia Scott, who didn't live to see
me published but always believed it would happen.*
  —Trina Wiebe

Goats Don't Brush Their Teeth
Text © 2002 Trina Wiebe
Illustrations © 2002 Marisol Sarrazin

Published by Lobster Press™
1620 Sherbrooke Street West, Suites C & D
Montréal, Québec   H3H 1C9
Tel. (514) 904-1100 • Fax (514) 904-1101 • www.lobsterpress.com

Publisher: Alison Fripp
Editor: Jane Pavanel
Cover design: Marielle Maheu
Inside layout: Maria Simpson

Distributed in the United States by:
Publishers Group West
1700 Fourth Street
Berkeley, CA 94710

Distributed in Canada by:
Raincoast Books
9050 Shaughnessey Street
Vancouver, BC V6P 6E5

We acknowledge the financial support of the Government of Canada through the Book
Publishing Industry Development Program (BPIDP) for our publishing activities.

We acknowledge the support of the Canada
Council for the Arts for our publishing program.

The Canada Council | Le Conseil des Arts
    for the Arts | du Canada

National Library of Canada Cataloguing in Publication Data

Wiebe, Trina, 1970-
    Goats don't brush their teeth

(Abby and Tess, pet-sitters, ISSN 1499-9412 ; 6)
ISBN 1-894222-59-8

    I. Pavanel, Jane, 1957- II. Sarrazin, Marisol, 1965- III. Title.
IV. Series: Wiebe, Trina, 1970- . Abby and Tess, pet-sitters ; 6.

PS8595.I358G63 2002   jC813'.6   C2002-900874-3
PR9199.3.W473G63 2002

Printed and bound in Canada

Contents

1 Buried Treasure

"Mom is going to be so mad," said Abby, staring at the floor.

Tess whimpered.

There was potting soil everywhere. Abby could see where Tess had stepped in it, grinding it into the beige carpet. In the middle of the mess was Mom's fig tree, leaning sideways in its round clay pot.

"You're in big trouble," she said. "You know Mom told you to stop digging in her plants."

"Woof." Tess scratched behind her left ear nervously, leaving a dirty smudge on her neck.

Abby sighed. Just when she thought she was used to her sister's odd ways, Tess did something like this. Abby was the only one in her whole school who had a little sister who thought she was a dog. It was annoying.

Mom, on the other hand, usually didn't mind when Tess acted more canine than human. Like when she left teeth marks in the morning paper or barked when someone knocked on the apartment door. But lately Mom had been kind of grouchy.

Mom taught art classes at the community center, but most of the time she could be found in her studio at the end of the hall, working on her latest painting. That's where she was now. At any moment she could walk in and discover the mess.

"All right," Abby grumbled, unable to resist her sister's sad, hangdog eyes. "I'll help you clean up before Mom sees it."

Abby knelt on the carpet and scraped the soil into a pile. It was soggy and clung to her fingers. This is going to leave an awful stain, she thought. She scooped it up and dumped it back into the pot.

"Why do you have to dig all the time?" she asked, exasperated. She straightened the tree and pressed the soil down around the base of its trunk.

Tess shrugged. "How else can I bury stuff?"

Abby froze. "Bury stuff?"

"Woof," barked Tess happily. "Dogs always bury their stuff. To keep it safe."

Abby looked at the pot and groaned. She dug through the soil until her fingers hit something hard. It was a set of keys.

"Tess," she wailed, "Mom's been looking all over for these!"

"For what?" asked Mom.

Abby spun around. "Oh, hi Mom," she said with a tentative smile. "Look what we found."

Mom's eyes went from the keys to the soiled carpet to Tess. "I see."

"Actually, I found them," piped up Tess. "They were in the laundry basket."

Mom sank into a nearby armchair. "The laundry basket?"

Tess barked and jumped up and down. "Yeah. I was digging under the clothes to hide my bone and I found them."

One of Tess's favorite possessions was a rubber chew toy in the shape of a bone. She loved to hide it. Sometimes Abby discovered it under her pillow or stuck in the sleeve of her housecoat. Once she'd even found it in the freezer, next to a carton of mint chocolate chip ice cream.

"You were digging in the dirty clothes," said Mom, rubbing her temples, "to hide your bone."

"Yup," Tess said with a wide grin. "I dug way down and there they were. Just like buried treasure."

Mom smiled weakly. "Amazing. But why are my keys muddy? And what happened to my plant?"

"Well, I was going to give them to you right away," Tess said, "but then I pretended I went to the park and I wanted to bury my bone under a bush, so . . ."

"You buried them too," Mom finished. Instead of getting angry, like Abby expected, her voice only sounded tired. She looked at the mess and shook her head.

"Sorry," said Tess.

"I know you've been bored since school let out," Mom said, glancing around the crowded apartment. "I wish we had a backyard for you to play in. But you can't dig in my houseplants, Tess. They won't survive the summer, and neither will

9

my carpet."

Abby noticed dark half-circles under Mom's eyes and wondered why she looked so tired. She felt a pang of concern, but forgot it when she heard Mom's next words.

"That's why your dad and I have decided to send you girls away for awhile."

2 Vacation Time

"Send us away?" cried Tess. "Like to the dog pound?"

Mom laughed, looking like her old self again. "No, silly. Your grandmother has invited you to spend next week with her. You'll have plenty of space to run around in," she smiled at Tess, "and you can dig all the holes you want."

Tess threw back her head and howled with delight. She danced around in circles, chanting, "We're going to Granny Ida's house, we're going to Granny Ida's house."

Abby didn't care about digging holes or having room to run. All she could think about was spending an entire week with her favorite person in the whole world.

Gran lived on a farm with a bunch of ducks and chickens and a friendly old dog named Toby. She loved animals almost as much as Abby did. Which was a lot. Abby wanted to be a veterinarian when she grew up. As far as she was concerned, there wasn't a better job in the world than taking care of animals all day.

Whenever Abby visited Gran she fed Toby and helped take care of the chickens and ducks. She pretended she lived on the farm and the animals belonged to her, instead of living in their dumb apartment with the strict No Pets Allowed rule.

Abby hated that rule. She had always longed for a puppy or a furry little kitten, but it looked like she'd never have a pet of her own. Then one day she'd come up with a brilliant idea, to pet-sit other people's animals! Since then, she and Tess had taken care of all kinds of pets . . . a hamster, a pot-bellied pig, even a colony of ants that belonged to a boy in her class. It was the perfect solution.

But spending time on Gran's farm was even better!

"Tess and I really get to stay with Gran for a week?" asked Abby. "Seven whole days?"

"Tomorrow Dad has a day off," Mom said. "We'll all drive down together."

"I need to pack," exclaimed Tess. She stopped spinning around the room and counted on her fingers. "I have to bring my rubber bone and my flea-bath shampoo and my leash and . . ."

"First you can finish cleaning up," Mom said with a smile. "Then you can pack. And don't forget to put some clothes in your suitcase."

Abby made a mental list of what she'd need to bring. Normal stuff, not pet supplies. Things like socks and T-shirts, and of course, her super-secret diary.

No one knew she kept a diary, not even Tess. This was pretty amazing considering how many times Abby had caught Tess poking through her belongings. It was hard to have privacy when you shared a room with your sister. Abby had to keep her diary hidden in the very back of her desk drawer, booby-trapped with a piece of thread.

Now she had a new problem. How could she get her diary to Gran's without Tess noticing? She'd have to smuggle it into her suitcase when Tess wasn't looking. I'll do it tonight, she decided, while Tess is in the bath, or maybe after she falls asleep.

"Oh, girls, I almost forgot," said Mom, breaking into Abby's thoughts. "Gran said to tell you she's got a surprise waiting for you."

Abby sucked in her breath. That could only mean one thing . . . a new animal!

3 The Open Road

Abby sat on her suitcase by the front door and checked her watch for the hundredth time.

7:05 a.m.

"When are they going to wake up?" she muttered. She tugged on the string she always wore around her neck. Usually it only held the apartment key, in case she and Tess were accidentally locked out, but today she'd added a second key. It opened the padlock on her blue suitcase. Her super-secret diary was hidden inside.

A door squeaked. Abby flew down the hall and collided with Dad in front of the bathroom.

"Morning," she said, grinning. "When do we hit the road?"

Dad groaned. His hair stuck up on one side and his striped pajamas were rumpled. He yawned and scratched his chin. "What's the rush?"

"What's the rush?" repeated Abby. She opened her mouth to protest, then closed it when she saw Dad's teasing grin.

"Don't worry," he said. "Gran's not expecting us at the crack of dawn."

"Yeah, but it's already after seven and Mom and Tess aren't even awake yet."

"Shhh." Dad glanced at his bedroom door. "Mom didn't sleep well last night. Look, I'll make you a deal. Let her stay in bed a little longer and I'll fix you breakfast."

"I already ate," grumbled Abby, "an hour ago."

Dad chuckled and stepped into the bathroom. "We'll be at Gran's before lunch. You have my word on it."

Abby rinsed and put away her breakfast dishes. She carried her suitcase outside and stowed it in the car trunk, then decided to run back and get Tess's suitcase too. Anything to speed up her slowpoke family.

An hour later everyone was finally settled in the car. Dad started the engine and pulled away from the curb.

They were on their way!

Abby watched the buildings whiz by. They

passed Mr. Nakama's pet store, the library and the school, then they traveled through street after street of tidy, newly built houses. Eventually they were out of town, driving between grassy green fields.

"I see a cow!" exclaimed Tess. She undid her seatbelt, knelt on the seat and rolled down the window. Panting eagerly, she leaned forward and closed her eyes, pointing her face into the wind. Her ponytails flapped wildly behind her.

"Buckle up, Tess," Mom ordered.

"Awww," pouted Tess. She crossed her arms and slumped back in her seat. "I like hanging out the window."

"Too bad," said Mom with a frown. "I want your seatbelt fastened every single time you . . ."

"Look," cried Abby, hoping to distract them. "More cows. And a horse!"

"Woof," barked Tess. She buckled her seatbelt and strained to see out the window. "Woof, woof!"

Abby gave a sigh of relief when Mom turned back to watch the road and Tess began

counting the livestock grazing in the fields. She didn't want anything to spoil her special day.

On and on they drove. Past barns and tractors and towering grain silos. Finally Dad turned into the familiar winding driveway and honked the car horn all the way up to the farmhouse.

Beep, beep! Beep, beep!

Dad switched off the engine and Abby flung open the passenger door. She raced across the lawn, straight into Gran's arms. Chickens clucked and fluttered out of the way.

"Ooof," said Gran as Tess barreled into her a few seconds later.

"I packed my own suitcase," Tess yipped, "and Mom said I could dig holes all day long."

Gran laughed and hugged her granddaughters. "Oh, it's good to see you!" she said. "It's been far too quiet around here."

Tess whooped and raced across the yard, barking at the top of her lungs. She galloped around the apple tree, startling Toby, who was blind in one eye. He loped toward Abby and Gran, Tess hot on his tail. He was getting on in years, but he still enjoyed a good game of chase. They disappeared behind the farmhouse.

Abby smiled. Back home the neighbors would have a fit if Tess ran around barking like a dog gone mad. But here on the farm there were no neighbors to complain and no building superintendent to complain to.

"Let's get your things into the house," suggested Gran. "I made a batch of buttermilk biscuits this morning."

Abby's mouth watered. She loved Gran's biscuits. They practically melted in your mouth. But there was something she needed to know first.

"What's the surprise?" she cried. "Is it a new animal?"

Gran smiled mysteriously. "Why don't you take a look around?"

4 Sniffing Around

Abby headed straight for the barn. It was big and old and painted a beautiful red. When Gramps was alive it had been full of cows. Now it just held gardening tools and chicken feed and bedding straw. If there was a new animal, that's where it would be.

A wooden corral fenced in the grassy area in front of the barn. Abby unlatched the gate and crossed the corral. She paused in front of the barn door, enjoying the tingle of anticipation that crept up her spine. Then she opened it and stepped inside.

Everything was just as she remembered it. The unpainted wooden walls were aged to a soft gray. Shovels and pitchforks and gardening tools hung neatly from nails pounded into the rough planks. Dusty sunbeams fell across the floor-boards.

"Here kitty, kitty," she called. She strained to hear an answering meow, but the barn was quiet. A kitten would be so wonderful. It would sleep at the end of her bed and purr when she stroked its fur. Toby was great, but he slept outdoors at night and spent most of his days looking for something to chase.

Abby took a few steps, then heard a soft scratching sound. "Don't be afraid," she crooned. "I won't hurt you."

She noticed a pile of straw in the first stall. The pile rustled, then was still. She tiptoed toward it, her hand outstretched. "Here kitty, kitty."

Suddenly the straw exploded. Abby threw up her arms to protect her face.

"Boo!" shouted Tess. She took one look at her terrified sister and collapsed in laughter.

"Are you crazy?" shouted Abby. "You just about scared me to death."

Tess sat up and hiccuped. "Wasn't that funny?"

"Hilarious," muttered Abby.

"I'm going to use my super sense of smell to help you find the surprise," said Tess, shaking bits of straw from her hair. "What do you think it is?"

Abby shrugged, although she was still hoping for a kitten. Or maybe a batch of fluffy baby chicks. "There's only one way to find out," she said. "Let's start looking."

But the storage room was empty. So was the hayloft and the area where Gramps had kept his milking equipment. The only signs of life they found were mouse droppings scattered behind a bag of chicken feed.

"I'm hungry," whined Tess.

"Gran made biscuits," Abby said, peering into each stall as they walked down the center of the barn. "You can go if you want, but I've got one more place to check."

The last stall was the largest. Gramps had used it during calving season, to keep an eye on cows about to give birth. Whatever Gran's surprise was, it had to be there.

Abby kept walking. The smell of fresh manure filled her nostrils. There was something there, all right. Tess yelped and covered her nose.

Abby smirked. Sometimes having a super sense of smell wasn't so fun after all. "I guess it's not a kitten," she said, her eyes watering as they reached the stall.

For once Tess didn't try to push past her. Instead, she scrambled up the gate, climbing the wooden rails like a ladder. Abby swung the gate open with Tess still clinging to it.

"Hey, look!" cried Tess. "I see . . ."

"I see it too," said Abby, her back to Tess. A bright blue cube lay in the straw. She stared at it, puzzled.

Tess tried again. "But Abby . . ."

"It looks like a giant building block," said Abby. She stepped forward and nudged it with her toe. "I've never seen . . ."

Just then something pinched her. Hard.

Abby shrieked and clutched the seat of her pants. She whirled around to yell at Tess, only it wasn't Tess playing tricks on her this time.

It was a goat.

"Baaah," it said.

"I tried to tell you," giggled Tess from her perch. She pointed to the far end of the stall. "Look."

Sleeping in the corner were two more goats. The one that had nipped Abby was much smaller than the others. It bleated softly.

"Goats," breathed Abby. "Gran has goats!"

The barn door creaked. They heard Gran clomping toward them in her rubber boots. When she reached the gate, she had a big smile on her face.

"I see you've found my surprise," she said. "That's Maisie and Gertie over there, and this little one is Gertie's kid."

"Kid?" Tess scrunched up her face. "She

doesn't look like a kid to me."

Abby spoke without taking her eyes off the small animal. "Baby goats are called kids. Everybody knows that."

"I haven't named her yet," said Gran. "She's already very tame, and quite intelligent too."

"Oh," said Abby, her eyes lighting up. "Can I name her? Please? I promise I'll find the perfect name."

"How about Pincher," suggested Tess with a sly grin. "Or Biter or Chomper?"

Gran chuckled. "Did she nip you, Abby? Goats are playful creatures. You have to keep an eye on them. But they can't hurt you too badly because they don't have any upper teeth."

Gertie's kid took a dainty step forward on its spindly legs. Abby watched it uneasily. Teeth or no teeth, this kid packed a powerful pinch.

The kid bleated and laid its head against Abby's leg. Abby gazed into its gentle brown eyes and completely forgot her sore rear end.

She was in love.

5 Packing Light

"What happened to their ears?" demanded Tess. She jumped off the gate and landed with a thud beside Gran. "Did they fall off?"

Gran chuckled. "No, dear. These are La Mancha goats. It's a Spanish breed. They're famous for their ears, or rather, their lack of ears."

Maisie and Gertie were awake now. They trotted over and crowded close to Gran. At first it did seem like they were earless, but when Abby looked closer she realized they had one small nub on each side of their head. Somehow, it made them even more special.

"I'm going to take good care of them," Abby said, scratching the kid just above her nose. "I'll feed them and bring them water and groom them . . ."

"And milk them," added Gran.

"Huh?" Abby wasn't sure she'd heard right. "Milk them?"

"They're dairy goats, dear. I make butter

and cheese from their milk. It's delicious on cereal too."

Abby gulped. For the first time she noticed that Gertie and Maisie had udders. In fact, they were hanging so low they almost touched the ground.

"Don't look so worried," said Gran with a laugh. "They don't need to be milked right away. I do that after supper and then again before breakfast. For now, why don't you and Tess help me get these critters outside. They've been cooped up all morning waiting for you to arrive."

Abby and Tess shooed the goats out of the barn and into the corral. Abby watched the kid run and jump. She couldn't wait to find just the right name for her. The perfect name. Maybe Mocha for the coffee-colored spot on her forehead?

"Okay, time to go, girls," said Gran. "Your parents want to say goodbye."

Tess raced ahead, but Abby waited while Gran carefully latched the gate. "I just love the goats," she said as they walked to the farmhouse.

"When did you get them?"

Gran looked thoughtful. "Just after Easter, I think. A few months ago. It was hard not to tell you about them over the phone, but I wanted to surprise you."

"They're the perfect surprise," Abby said. She slipped her arm through Gran's. "I'm so glad you invited us. Mom's been in such a grouchy mood lately. It'll be way more fun here with the goats. And with you," she added quickly.

Gran squeezed her hand. "Your mom's been working too hard lately," she said. "She needs a break. Besides, it'll be nice to have a few extra hands around here. The rooster crows at sunrise, remember? We've got to feed the chickens and ducks, milk the goats, weed the garden . . ."

"I thought this was supposed to be a vacation," joked Abby.

They were still smiling when they walked into Gran's kitchen. The walls were painted a sunny yellow and potted herbs filled the windowsills. Tess was already at the table seated between Mom and Dad.

"These are delicious," Tess said, cramming a biscuit into her mouth.

"Don't talk with your mouth full," criticized Abby. "Did you forget to pack your manners?"

"You're not the boss of me," sputtered Tess, peppering the tablecloth with crumbs. She wiped her mouth on her sleeve.

Mom shot them a warning look. "Knock it off, girls."

"Sorry," muttered Abby automatically.

"Speaking of packing, your suitcase was suspiciously light, Tess," said Dad.

Tess blinked.

Mom raised one eyebrow. "You packed the clothes I set out on your bed last night, right? The pajamas and socks and underwear . . ."

"I've got everything I need," Tess said.

Mom groaned. "Bring your suitcase here."

"But . . ." protested Tess.

"Now," Mom ordered, her voice firm.

Abby popped a piece of biscuit into her mouth and watched Tess march down the hall to the front door. She returned a moment later dragging her suitcase behind her.

Mom picked it up and frowned. She unzipped it and looked inside. Tess sidled over to Gran, watching Mom out of the corner of her eye.

"Don't worry if she forgot a few things," said Gran, putting her arm around Tess's shoulders. "There's that great used clothing store on King Street."

"She'll need more than a few things." Mom's voice sounded funny, like she didn't know whether to laugh or cry. "This is all Tess brought to wear for the whole week!"

Mom held up a white bathing suit with black spots. It was Tess's favorite piece of clothing. When she wore it she liked to pretend she was

Sparky, the Dalmatian that had visited her class during fire safety week.

"I needed room for my Boo Boo," Tess explained, pointing at her worn stuffed monkey. "I didn't want him to get squished."

Abby waited for Mom to explode, but she just dropped the bathing suit back into the suitcase. "She can't wear that thing all week," she said wearily.

"Don't worry," said Gran. "We'll find something for her in town tomorrow."

Dad stood up and clapped his hands. "Well, we should probably get going. We've got a bit of a drive ahead of us."

Abby grinned and jumped to her feet. She'd miss her parents, but she couldn't wait for this vacation to begin. She had so many things to do. Unpack her suitcase, collect the eggs, help Gran in the garden. Best of all, she had a baby goat to name!

6 A Dream Come True

"Why don't you girls get settled in your rooms," Gran said when Mom and Dad were gone.

"You mean room," corrected Abby. She and Tess always shared the guest room down the hall from the kitchen, unless Mom and Dad stayed the night too. When that happened Abby and Tess slept on the pull-out couch in the living room.

"No," said Gran, "that's my other surprise. I had the attic renovated into a bedroom. What do you think of that?"

"I get a room to myself?" Abby could hardly believe her ears. "Which one?"

Gran chuckled. "Why don't you take the new room, Abby? Go and see what you think."

Instead of heading to the attic, Abby flew at Gran and hugged her. "This is going to be the best vacation ever!"

"Easy now," said Gran, laughing. "Tess, the

guest room is all yours. You can use the dresser for your, uh, bathing suit."

"Okay," Tess mumbled. She clutched Boo Boo under one arm and dragged her suitcase down the hall.

Abby forgot about the crestfallen look on Tess's face as she pulled down the ladder that led to the attic. Using one hand, she climbed as fast as she could, her suitcase bumping into her legs with every rung. She was getting her own room!

It was perfect.

In the corner was a polished brass bed covered with a patchwork quilt. Framed needlepoint pictures hung on the wall. The wooden dresser that stood near the bed held photos of Gran and Gramps and the whole family.

Abby twirled around slowly, loving the flowered wallpaper Gran had chosen. The sloped ceilings made the room seem warm and cozy. And private. She sighed with delight. Up here she could do anything she wanted.

She set her suitcase on the bed and went over to the window. A wide seat was built beneath it, perfect for curling up with a good book. Outside Abby could see the barn and the duck pond. She watched the kid poke her head through the corral fence to nibble sweet wild clover growing on the other side.

"Clover," said Abby, testing the name out loud. "That might be just right for you."

"We're going outside now," Gran called. "Everything okay up there?"

"Everything's great," Abby called back. Actually, it was more than great. It was a dream come true. She glanced around the tidy room and sighed happily. For once she didn't have to worry about stepping on her sister's toys or tripping over dirty clothes.

Abby unlocked her suitcase and arranged her clothes in the dresser. Then she pulled out her super-secret diary. She longed to settle into the window seat and start writing, but Gran was waiting. She put her diary on the night table, gave it a pat, then hurried downstairs.

Gran was on her knees in the garden, thinning carrots. "How's the room?" she asked.

"I love it," said Abby. She knelt in the warm soil beside Gran and pulled up a baby carrot that was wedged between two bigger ones. Abby had helped Gran in the garden many times and knew how important it was to give the stronger plants enough room to grow.

"Woof!" Tess leapt out from behind a giant rhubarb plant. She was wearing her spotted bathing suit.

"Would you quit doing that?" demanded Abby, tossing the baby carrot onto the weed pile. She pulled up another one. "Every time I turn around you jump out at me. Can't you think of anything better to do?"

Tess growled and kicked the weed pile. "Can I play in your room sometime?"

Abby sat back on her heels. "Why would you want to? You've got the guest room all to yourself."

"It's boring," Tess whined. "I like it better when we're together. Can I sleep up there too?"

Abby stared at her sister. For the first time in her life she had complete privacy. She didn't

have to booby-trap her diary. She could write in it any time she liked, instead of sneaking to the bathroom or waiting until Tess was asleep.

"Sometimes a person needs privacy," Gran said, seeing the distress on Abby's face. "When you get older you'll understand. You'll want to keep secrets too."

"Secrets are dumb," Tess snorted. "Anyway, Abby doesn't have any secrets."

Abby frowned. "For your information, I do too," she said. "Just because we're sisters doesn't mean I have to share everything with you."

Two angry pink dots popped up on Tess's cheeks. "Yeah, well, I have secrets too! Hundreds of them. And they're way better than yours."

"Why don't we run into town for some ice cream," Gran interrupted. "Afterwards we can pick up some clothes for Tess."

"I don't want any clothes and I don't care about Abby's mean old secrets," shouted Tess. She stomped across the garden. Soil flew through the air as she began digging a hole.

"Oh dear." Gran rose to her feet with a groan. "I'd better rescue my beets."

Abby yanked up another carrot. It was normal to want to keep some things secret. Even Gran said so. A week of privacy was going to be heaven.

Why was Tess making such a fuss?

7 No Sisters Allowed

"Where's my sparkle pen?" cried Abby the next morning. She dropped to her knees and peered under the picnic table that took up most of the front porch.

She'd been writing a letter to Dirk, the boy with the ants. They were pretty good friends now. Not girlfriend-boyfriend, thought Abby quickly, just friends. Anyway, she'd stopped writing when Gran had called her inside to help set the table for breakfast. Now the pen was gone and so was the letter.

"Gran," she called, sticking her head into the kitchen. "Have you seen my pen and my letter anywhere?"

Gran looked up from the stove. "No, dear, but I'm sure they're around here somewhere. They didn't grow legs and walk away."

Abby frowned. Maybe they'd disappeared with a little help. She stormed through the kitchen and down the hall. Not bothering to knock, she threw open the guest room door.

It was a disaster zone. The bed was stripped and blankets and sheets were draped over the dresser. It looked like Tess was in the middle of one of her favorite projects — building a tent. Abby was glad she wasn't sharing a room with her. What a mess!

"Tess?" she addressed the tent, "are you in there?"

"Go away."

Abby picked her way across the floor and lifted the corner of a sheet. "Did you take my sparkle pen?"

Tess frowned. "No."

"I just had it a minute ago. Are you sure you didn't touch it?" She'd seen Tess admiring the pen earlier. The top half was filled with water and sparkles. When you gave it a shake, it looked like a magic wand.

"No. Go away." Tess crawled out of her tent. "This is my room. No sisters allowed. I need my privacy, you know."

Abby bit back a nasty retort. She'd more or

less said the same thing yesterday. "Are you ever going to change your clothes?" she asked instead.

"Never," Tess replied stubbornly. She was wearing her bathing suit again. The clothes Gran had bought for her hung in the closet, untouched.

Tess reached into the tent and pulled out her monkey and a small book. "Come on, Boo Boo. We've got stuff to do. Secret stuff," she added as she tried to brush past her sister.

"Hey," cried Abby. "That looks like my diary!"

Tess stared at Abby like she'd lost her mind. "What diary?"

Abby grabbed at the book but Tess clutched it to her chest. "What are you doing?" cried Tess. "This is my new notebook! I found it, it's mine!"

"It's not yours," shouted Abby, tugging on the diary. She twisted hard and jerked it loose from Tess's grip. "Just where exactly did you find it?"

Tess's face grew pink. "Somewhere."

Abby waved the book in front of Tess's eyes. "Somewhere like my room, that's where. I told you not to go up there. You invaded my privacy!"

Tess's eyes filled with tears. "I don't know why you're getting so crazy over a dumb notebook," she said. "It's just filled with scribbles."

"They're not scribbles," Abby practically screamed. "They're my secret . . ." She stopped and took a deep breath. Not only had Tess invaded her space, but the diary contained all of

Abby's innermost thoughts. Thoughts about school and family . . . and boys. Or rather, one boy in particular who liked ants.

Abby gulped. Thank goodness Tess couldn't read. "Who did you show this to?" she demanded.

"Nobody," Tess replied. "What's so special about it, anyway?"

"Nothing," said Abby quickly. "I'm just mad because you sneaked into my room. If you do that again, I'll phone Mom. Would you like that?"

Tess's eyes grew wide. "No."

"I mean it," threatened Abby. "She'd probably come right out here to take you home . . ."

"What's the big deal?" cried Tess. "I just wanted to see what your dumb room looked like. You're such a meanie!" She turned and ran from the room. Five seconds later the front door slammed.

Weirdo, Abby thought, smoothing a corner of the diary that had gotten bent in the struggle. She meant it. Tess had been acting strange lately. She used to follow Abby everywhere, but now she disappeared every morning until lunch.

And she was acting like a dog more than ever, digging holes all over the yard.

Still angry, Abby went to examine her room. Everything was exactly the same, but somehow it felt different. Definitely less private.

Abby knew she couldn't leave her diary out in the open anymore. Grimly, she fished her suitcase out from under the bed. She put her diary inside and locked it up tight using the tiny key on the string around her neck.

Her secrets were safe again.

8 Milking Lessons

Frowning, Abby wandered into the kitchen and sat at the table. Gran piled some scrambled eggs onto her plate.

"Cheer up," said Gran. "I lose things all the time."

Abby's heart stopped. Did Gran know about her secret diary? Had Tess lied about not showing it to her? "What are you talking about?" she finally asked.

"Why, your pen and letter, of course," said Gran. "What did you think I was talking about?"

"Oh, nothing," said Abby. She began shoveling eggs into her mouth. "These are yummy, Gran."

"Farm fresh," said Gran with a smile. "Listen, how about a trip to town after chores? Mineral blocks are on sale."

"Yeah, sure," said Abby, jabbing her fork into the eggs. She'd agree to anything as long as the word "diary" didn't come up. Then she stopped and looked at Gran. "Mineral blocks?"

"I need an extra one for the goats," said Gran. "You must have seen their old one."

"That gigantic blue building block?" Abby asked.

"That's right," Gran said. "The goats don't get all the nutrition they need from the dry feed, so I give them a mineral block to lick. Keeps them healthy."

"So it's like a vitamin popsicle," Abby joked, "except it's not cold."

Gran chuckled. "Exactly. Okay, smarty-pants. How are goats the same as cows?"

"They both give milk," said Abby.

"True," said Gran, "but that's not what I'm thinking of."

"They both have two eyes?" asked Abby, "and four legs?"

"Guess again," said Gran.

Abby thought for a moment. Gran had let her take a pile of goat books up to bed last night. She remembered reading something special that had reminded her of cows, but she couldn't think what it was.

"I give up," she finally said.

"They both chew their cud when they rest," said Gran.

"I remember now," agreed Abby. "And goats are kind of like deer because the males are called bucks and females are called does. Maybe I should name the kid Bambi."

"Still haven't decided on a name?" asked Gran.

Abby shook her head. "I can't find one that's just right."

"Well, there's plenty of time yet," Gran said, heading out the door. "I'm going to get started on the chores."

"I'll be there in a minute." Abby dug into her eggs. She'd worry about the pen and letter later. Today Gran had promised to teach her how to milk a goat.

Ten minutes later Abby was in the barn, seated on the three-legged milking stool.

"Go ahead," said Gran. "Give it a try."

"Okay," said Abby. How hard could it be?

She studied Gertie's udder, trying to decide which teat to take. Nervously, she chose the closest one and squeezed.

Nothing happened.

She tugged, then tugged again. Still nothing. She squeezed and tugged at the same time, but not a single drop of milk came out.

"Like this," Gran said, reaching over and taking a teat between her thumb and two fingers. She coaxed the milk out in a smooth, rhythmic motion. Then it was Abby's turn. Concentrating hard, she finally managed to produce a few drops. They plinked into the metal bucket.

"I did it!" Abby exclaimed. She'd have lots to write about in her diary tonight. She wished she had her sparkle pen. It wasn't the same writing with one of Gran's old pencils. Slowly, a pool of milk formed in the bottom of the pail.

Gertie gazed contentedly over her shoulder at Abby. Then she lifted her back right hoof and gave the bucket a sharp kick.

"Hey!" cried Abby as the bucket tipped and all her hard work soaked into the barn floor.

Gran laughed. "Goats can sure be unpredictable," she said. "I'll finish up. You find Tess and see if she's ready to head into town."

"All right. I can tell when I'm not wanted," grumbled Abby. She stuck out her tongue at Gertie and let Gran have the stool. Soon the milk was plink-plink-plinking into the bucket in a steady rhythm.

The kid trotted over and pushed her nose into Abby's pocket. Abby smiled. These days when she came to the barn, she always brought a little treat with her.

"How about a nice crunchy apple?" she asked. "Here you go, Cinnamon. Or do you prefer Nutmeg?" She scratched the small goat between her shoulder blades.

When the apple was gone Abby kissed the kid's forehead and left to look for Tess. I hope she's easy to find this time, she thought crossly. As she neared the farmhouse she spotted a familiar figure crouched in the flowerbed.

"Woof, woof," yipped Tess. "I found buried treasure!"

Abby eyed the objects in her sister's hand and groaned. "Tess, you're ruining the flowers Gran planted."

"These aren't flowers. I know what flowers look like, silly." Tess gave a snort. "These are round and hard and brown. I bet they have gold nuggets inside."

Abby was just about to reply when she heard Gran's footsteps behind her.

"Tess," Gran gasped, "why did you dig up my tulip bulbs?"

"Bulbs?" Tess's shoulders slumped. "You mean they're not buried treasure?"

"Well, in a way they are," Gran said, setting the bucket of milk on the porch. "A bulb is a lot like buried treasure because it stays in the ground until it blooms in the spring. But if you dig them up now we won't have any tulips next year."

"Sorry," mumbled Tess.

"Why don't we replant them together," Gran suggested.

Gran and Tess dropped the bulbs into the ground with their pointy ends up. Then they covered them with dirt. "Maybe this isn't the best place to dig holes," Gran said to Tess when they were done.

"That's what you said about the garden," Tess complained. "You said I was worse than a gopher."

"Well, you did dig up my beets. And some of my turnips," said Gran, putting her hands on her hips. "Which reminds me, have you seen a purple gardening glove? I'm sure I left both gloves near the rhubarb yesterday, but one is missing. It seems to have walked off by itself."

Tess giggled. "That's funny."

Abby smiled too. Gran was always losing her reading glasses or forgetting things. Just this morning Abby had found the jam by the telephone and the message pad in the refrigerator.

It was all part of the fun of visiting Gran!

9   Too Many Secrets

Abby woke early the next day, just as the sky was beginning to lighten. She lay in bed listening to the familiar creaks and groans of the farmhouse.

Yawning, she reached for the key string draped over her bedpost. She dragged her suitcase out from under her bed, unlocked it and took out her diary. Wrapping herself in the quilt, she curled up in the window seat.

She flipped to the first empty page and pressed the point of her pencil to the paper. But before she could write a single word, a movement out the window caught her eye.

Something was in the grass near the duck pond.

Abby blinked and leaned forward. Could it be a coyote? Did coyotes eat goats?

She was about to race downstairs and wake up Gran when the animal moved out of the grass. It wasn't a coyote, it was a goat. A small goat with a chocolate-brown spot on its forehead.

"How'd you get out?" she whispered, angry and relieved at the same time. She tossed the quilt on her bed and jumped into her slippers. She had to get the kid back into the safety of the barn. Maybe there was no coyote, but what if she fell into the pond and drowned? Or wandered away from the farm and got lost?

"Someone must have left the gate open," she muttered as she hurried down the attic ladder. But who? Abby always double-checked the gate after she did her chores, so it couldn't have been her. Tess liked collecting the eggs in the morning, but she never went into the barn after dark. Which ruled her out too.

That left Gran.

Abby shook her head. Sure, Gran complained about how absentminded she was getting, but she took good care of her animals. Gran would never forget something this important.

Or would she?

Abby tiptoed across the yard, her slippers squelching with every step. The grass was soaked with dew, and by the time she reached the pond so were the cuffs of her pajama bottoms.

"Come on," she whispered to the kid. It looked at her but didn't move.

"Let's go," Abby tried again. "Don't you want some breakfast?"

As if it understood, the kid ripped up a mouthful of grass and began chewing. Abby frowned and took one step forward. The kid took one step back. Abby took another step forward and the kid retreated again.

"I know you like it out here," said Abby in what she hoped was a soothing voice, "but it's not safe. You need to be in the barn at night." She advanced several steps, keeping her eyes fixed on the kid's head. Finally, when she was close enough, she lunged. The kid tried to spring away but Abby was quicker.

"Gotcha," cried Abby.

Keeping a firm grip on the kid, Abby led her back to the barn. The corral gate was ajar. She noticed the barn door was open too.

Frowning, she filled a bucket with grain

and led the kid to her stall. Abby dumped the grain into the trough beside the mineral block, then checked to make sure the goats hadn't kicked over their water pail during the night. When she left the barn she triple-checked all the latches.

Abby paused outside. It was incredibly peaceful here. She could understand why Gran refused to move to town, even after Gramps died. With a sigh, she headed for the farmhouse.

"Good morning, dear," said Gran when Abby walked into the kitchen.

"Morning," Abby answered. She helped herself to some orange juice. "I fed the goats."

Gran jiggled the lever on the toaster. "Wonderful. You didn't spot my gardening glove, did you? I wanted to work in the garden later."

Abby bit her lip and shook her head. She'd forgotten about the glove.

"Oh well, I'm sure it'll turn up. I swear I'm growing more scatterbrained every day." Gran chuckled. "So, do you feel like making soap today?"

"Soap?"

Gran buttered her toast and nodded. "My goat milk soap is one of the best sellers at the Farmers' Market. Every weekend I set up a booth. I could use some help taking care of the customers if you'd like to earn a little money."

"Count me in," Abby said. She took her juice to the table and slid into her seat beside Tess.

"Can I help make soap too?" asked Tess. She swallowed the last spoonful of her cereal, then lapped up the milk left in the bottom of her bowl.

"Of course," said Gran, patting Tess on the head. "The more the merrier."

Abby ate her cereal, then cleared away the breakfast things while Gran brought out the soap-making ingredients. Soon the table held a jug of icy goat milk, several small bottles filled with colorful liquids, and jars of olive, coconut and palm oil.

"Woof," Tess yelped, jerking her nose away from one of the bottles. She quickly screwed the lid back on. "Pee-yoo."

"Those are essential oils," explained Gran. "A few drops will scent an entire batch of soap. They're not meant to be sniffed directly from the bottle."

Tess pulled the front of her bathing suit up over her nose. "Do I have to stay?"

Abby rolled her eyes. Tess's bathing suit had a blotchy red stain on it from their spaghetti supper last night.

"No, dear," said Gran, "but keep out of my flower beds, okay?"

"Yeah, okay." Tess grabbed Boo Boo and headed for the door.

"Where are you going?" demanded Abby. Tess was hardly around anymore. For some reason, it was starting to annoy Abby.

"I can't tell you." Tess stuck out her tongue. "It's a secret."

10 Boil and Bubble

"You're about to see an amazing chemical reaction," said Gran, drawing the milk jug closer.

Abby studied the equipment Gran had put on the table. There was a heavy-duty thermometer, various stainless steel utensils, safety goggles and a pair of yellow rubber gloves. It looked like a scientist's laboratory.

"I use lye," explained Gran. She moved the olive oil aside and looked behind the coconut oil. "Its scientific name is sodium hydroxide."

Abby watched Gran search the table, then open the cupboards above the stove. "It's a very caustic alkali," said Gran, peering in the lower cupboards. "It will make the milk quite hot, and when it cools we'll add the rest of the ingredients."

"What are you looking for?" asked Abby.

Gran pulled her head out from under the sink. "The lye. I thought I put it on the table."

"What does it look like?"

"It's in a small tin can," said Gran.

"A silver can?" asked Abby. "With a red lid?"

"That's it," cried Gran. "Where is it?"

"In the mailbox," said Abby, watching Gran closely. "I saw it there yesterday and meant to ask you what it was, but I forgot."

Gran looked surprised. "In the mailbox? How strange." She gave a little laugh. "Why Abby, you look so serious. It's okay, I do silly things like this all the time."

Wearing a worried frown, Abby ran to the mailbox at the end of the driveway. When she got back, she handed the lye to Gran without a word.

The soap-making process began. Carefully, Gran scooped several whitish beads out of the can and added them to the milk. Abby watched as Gran stirred and stirred. After a while the beads disappeared.

Gran nodded to the window above the sink. "Would you open that, dear? You won't smell anything, but lye produces fumes that can be quite dangerous."

Abby hurried to the window. I wish Gran

had remembered to tell me that before she added the lye, she thought.

"Okay," said Gran, "let's give it some time to cool."

Several minutes later Gran poured the lye-milk mixture into a blender. Then she added a small amount each of olive, coconut and palm oil. Next she added three drops of the peppermint oil Abby had picked. Finally she put the lid on firmly and turned the blender to its lowest speed.

The soap whirled around and around until Gran announced it was ready. Slowly, she poured it into molds she had greased earlier. She smoothed the tops with a knife and gently laid a sheet of clear plastic wrap over each mold.

"We'll set these aside overnight so they can harden," said Gran. "Tomorrow we'll pop them out and stack them up to dry. A month from now they'll be ready for market."

"A month?" said Abby with dismay. "But I'll be gone by then."

"They have to age before we can sell them," said Gran. "But don't worry, I've got

enough soap for this weekend. You can help me wrap them up, if you like."

Just then the kitchen door flew open and Tess burst into the room. She was filthy.

The white parts of her bathing suit weren't white anymore. Dirt and leaves clung to both knees. Her arms were muddy right up to her elbows, and something green and slimy was smeared across one cheek.

"Woof," barked Tess, waving a hand in the air. "I found a dinosaur bone!"

Abby couldn't make out what Tess was holding, but she knew it had never belonged to a dinosaur. "That's ridiculous," she said. "What makes you think . . ."

Then the stench hit her. Tess smelled rotten. Rotten like old potato peelings, shriveled apple cores and decaying lettuce leaves. "Oh, Tess," she gasped, holding her nose. "You stink!"

"Didn't you hear me?" cried Tess. "I dug up a dinosaur bone. A fossil! A real treasure!"

"Oh dear!" sighed Gran. "Please don't tell me you've been digging in my compost heap."

Tess looked at the bone in her hand. "You mean it's not a fossil?"

"I'm sorry, sweetie," Gran said, "it's just a chicken bone from the soup I made last week. It must have gotten mixed up with the vegetable peelings, then thrown in the compost. You really shouldn't play in there. It's full of bacteria."

Abby giggled. "And you thought the essential oils smelled bad," she said.

Gran herded Tess toward the bathroom. "I may be smelly," Tess shouted over her shoulder, "but I have the best secret in the whole world. And I'm not telling you. Not ever!"

11 Soap, Spies and Secrets

Abby helped Gran with the chores every day. She didn't try milking again, but she fed the chickens and ducks, helped collect the eggs and made sure the goats always had grain, clean straw and fresh water.

She spent hours with the kid, grooming it with Toby's dog brush, making its coat shine. Before long the kid was following her around the corral like a puppy, begging for a snack or a good long belly scratch.

Life on the farm is great, thought Abby. Even though she never did find her pen. Or Gran's gardening glove. Or her letter to Dirk. She was also missing a sock. One minute it was hanging on the clothesline, the next it was gone. And Tess still disappeared every day for hours.

Finally it was Friday. Abby was excited and sad at the same time. She couldn't wait to help Gran at the Farmers' Market, but she also knew that when the weekend was over, so was the visit.

"Pass the red ribbon, please," said Abby. She and Gran were sitting at the picnic table wrapping bars of soap. Tess, as usual, was nowhere to be found.

Gran rummaged in the basket beside her elbow and handed Abby a spool of shiny ribbon. Abby snipped off a piece and wound it around the bar of Honey Almond soap she'd just wrapped. She tied it and admired her work.

"Lovely," approved Gran.

Abby stacked the soap on top of the pile and grabbed a new one. "They do look good," she agreed. "We're almost ready for the market tomorrow."

"Baaa." A moist nose nudged Abby's elbow.

"Well, hi there, Dandelion," Abby said, trying out a new name. "How did you get out of the corral?"

The kid nuzzled Abby's wrist and bleated again.

"Maybe I left the gate open when I was mucking out the stalls," said Gran with a laugh. "That one gets into everything. Why, I caught her nibbling the laundry on the clothesline yesterday."

"I wish we didn't have to go home so soon. I'm going to miss her," Abby said, reaching into her pocket for a sugar cube. The goat eagerly crunched the cube and nuzzled her hand for more.

"Just think how much your parents must miss you," said Gran, wrapping another bar of soap. "And don't forget your pet-sitting job. I'm sure you want to get back to that."

"Yeah," Abby admitted. "I'm hoping to get some good jobs this summer."

"I'm sure you will," said Gran. She set the bar down and looked through her basket. "Did you use the silver ribbon?"

"Nope," said Abby. "Are you sure you've got silver?" she asked timidly, not wanting to hurt Gran's feelings. "Maybe you're mixed up . . ."

"I'm quite sure I bought a brand new spool last week. Perhaps it fell on the porch," suggested Gran.

Abby crouched down and looked under the picnic table. She found herself nose to nose with Boo Boo.

Tess peeked out from behind the stuffed monkey and flashed a smile. "Woof."

"Have you been here the whole time?" demanded Abby. "Don't you know it's rude to eavesdrop?"

"We're spies," Tess said. "That's how we get our best secrets." She reached behind her ear and grabbed an imaginary pencil. Pursing her lips, she scribbled in an invisible notebook. "I write them all down in my own special notebook. It's way better than your silly old diary," she added, wrinkling her nose in disgust.

"What are you talking about?" asked Abby, but Tess only smiled and scampered away. Abby watched her disappear behind the chicken coop.

"Never mind. I'll use this blue ribbon instead," said Gran. "Why don't you put the kid back in the corral. I'll finish up here."

Abby hesitated, then stood up. She looked around, but the kid had wandered off. With a shake of her head, Abby set out to find her. Tess, the kid, the ribbon . . . suddenly everything seemed to be disappearing.

12 To Market, To Market

"Where's my toothbrush?" grumbled Abby the next morning.

Gran poked her head into the bathroom. "What, dear?"

Abby pointed at the toothbrush holder beside the sink. "My toothbrush is gone."

"Never mind that," Gran said. "We've got to leave now if we want to set up before the crowds come. Run and get your sister."

"But my teeth . . ." Abby turned around but the doorway was empty. She ran down the hall and barged into the guest room. "Tess, did you see my toothbrush?"

Tess crawled out of her tent. "Nope."

Abby groaned. "I need to brush my teeth!"

Tess consulted her invisible notebook. "I didn't touch your yucky old toothbrush," she said, pretending to flip through her notes. "But I bet I know who did."

Abby heard the truck's engine growl to life.

"Who?" she demanded.

Tess pretended to lock her lips. Then she dropped the imaginary key down the front of her bathing suit. "It's a secret," she said smugly.

"You and your secrets," muttered Abby. For a fleeting moment she wondered if Gran could have misplaced the toothbrush when she was tidying the bathroom. Mom was always saying she worried about Gran living out here by herself. What if she was right? Little things like gardening gloves and toothbrushes didn't matter, but what if Gran misplaced her blood pressure medication or forgot to take Toby for his check-up at the vet?

Honk! Honk!

Abby pushed away her uneasy thoughts and ran outside after Tess. She flicked her tongue over her fuzzy teeth and frowned. She'd have to think about this later.

The market bustled with activity. A fat man in a white apron was busy setting up his hot dog stand. Three musicians stood on a stage tuning their instruments. A teenaged girl was busy at the pony rides, grooming a handsome brown pony. Everybody was getting ready for the crowds that would soon come. It was so exciting that Abby completely forgot her worries.

"Let's get ready," said Gran. "We don't have much time."

Abby, Tess and Gran worked together, carrying boxes of soap from the truck and arranging them prettily on the table. They finished just as the first customers arrived.

Tess quickly grew bored behind the booth. She wandered over to watch the pony rides, then went to get her face painted. Abby didn't mind. She and Tess weren't on speaking terms anyway.

Abby smiled and talked to people and soon she was selling soap like she'd been doing it all her life. Morning turned into afternoon, and before she realized it the market was closing and it was time to pack up.

"Are you rich now, Gran?" asked Tess as they drove home.

Gran laughed. "We did very well. We sold all the Honey Oatmeal soaps and there are only a few Lavender ones left. Your sister is a natural saleswoman."

Abby yawned. She was exhausted and her cheeks ached from smiling. She'd worked hard today, but it felt good. Luckily, the three apple fritters she'd eaten for lunch had taken away the stale, fuzzy feeling in her mouth.

Abby fiddled with the radio dial and found a station that was playing some familiar songs. She and Gran began singing along, loudly and off-key. They were almost home when Tess clutched the dashboard. "Stop!" she screamed.

Gran slammed on the brakes. In the middle of the road stood Maisie, Gertie and the kid.

"How did they get here?" cried Abby. "They could have been killed!" In a flash she was out of the truck and shooing the goats into the ditch.

Tess stuck her head through the open door. "I bet I know . . ."

"Not now," snapped Abby. She grabbed a handful of grass and coaxed the goats up the other side of the ditch and into Gran's field.

"There's no need to get excited," Gran said in a calm voice. "No harm done."

Abby couldn't help herself. "No harm done? If we hadn't stopped in time . . ." She bit her lip, unable to finish her thought.

"Why don't you walk the rest of the way," Gran suggested. "The goats will follow you. I'm sure they're hungry for their supper."

Gran was right. The goats followed Abby across the field, through the corral and into the barn. All of Abby's worries returned, only they seemed ten times worse now.

Had Gran forgotten to latch the corral gate? Was it dangerous for her to be alone on the farm? But this was Gran's home! What if she had to leave? What would happen to the animals?

The goats seemed to sense how upset Abby was. Even the kid stayed away as Abby slammed the grain bucket around and mumbled under her breath. When everyone was fed and watered she headed back to the farmhouse.

Gran met her on the front porch with the milk pail in her hand. "Don't worry, dear, the goats are fine. I'll just have to be more careful in the future."

Abby sucked in her breath. "You think you forgot to close the gate?"

"Oh, probably. It's not the first time this has happened, you know. Maybe I'm getting too old to be doing this . . ." Her voice trailed off and Abby saw a trace of sadness in her eyes. Then Gran blinked. "By the way, did you close the kitchen door behind you this morning? It was wide open when Tess and I drove into the yard."

"Of course I did," Abby said, glancing across the porch at the door. It was shut now. "Maybe Tess . . ."

"Tess wasn't the last person out of the house," Gran said. "You were. At least I remember that much."

Gran was right. Abby had been the last one out. But she was certain she'd closed the door behind her. She remembered because the farmhouse was old and you had to give the door a shove before it clicked shut. Nobody locked their doors around here, but she'd definitely heard the click.

Hadn't she?

13   Nobody's Perfect

"You're getting as addle-brained as I am," said Gran with a little smile. She gave Abby's arm a gentle squeeze before she continued to the barn.

Abby stared at the farmhouse door. Could she really have left it open? Maybe she hadn't shoved it hard enough. She was still trying to remember when she caught a flash of white out of the corner of her eye.

Tess.

Tess crept out of the shadows and darted across the yard, then slipped into the barn. Abby frowned. Was she spying on Gran now too?

"This is crazy," Abby muttered. It was time to figure out what Tess was up to. Tiptoeing along the path, she followed her sister through the corral.

The barn lights glowed softly. Abby stepped inside and heard Gran humming as she milked Gertie. But where was Tess?

A wisp of hay drifted down from the ceiling.

The hayloft! Gran never used it. With just three goats, it was easier to store the straw in an empty stall, close at hand. Abby and Tess had searched the loft on their first day here and all they had found were several forgotten bales of hay.

Abby climbed the ladder without making a sound. Peering over the top rung, she saw that the hayloft had been transformed into the perfect spy headquarters.

Tess had dragged a couple of the bales into the center of the floor for seats. An overturned wooden crate served as a table and a circular spot had been rubbed clean in the middle of a dusty window. Abby climbed the last few rungs and walked over to the window. She could see the whole yard from up here.

"What are you doing?"

Startled, Abby whirled around. Tess and Boo Boo stepped out from behind a large bale.

"You're sneaking through my stuff," accused Tess.

"I'm not . . ." began Abby. She felt a pang

of guilt and stopped. She *was* poking around in Tess's private space.

"You had a big hairy fit when I went into your room," said Tess, "so you can't come up here. No sisters allowed."

Abby looked at Tess. She seemed so small and lonely, standing there clutching her battered monkey like he was her last friend in the world. Maybe Abby shouldn't have made such a big deal about keeping Tess out of her room. It wasn't so bad keeping her diary locked in the suitcase. Why had she been so stubborn?

"Tess," she began.

"You're a dirty sneak," yelled Tess. "You said spying was bad, but you're spying on me!"

Abby swallowed and tried to explain. "I was just trying to figure out what was going on. I'm worried about Gran. I didn't realize this was your secret place."

Tess stared at Abby for a moment, then stomped over to the ladder and climbed down without saying a word.

14 An Amazing Discovery

Abby climbed down the ladder and wandered over to where Gran was milking Gertie.

"Everything okay?" Gran asked. "I heard shouting."

Abby shrugged. "I didn't know she had a secret hideout up there."

"But you poked around anyway?"

Abby stared at her feet. "Yeah. I wanted to know where she disappeared to all the time."

"Tess plays up there every day," Gran said, "all by herself." Gran stopped milking and brushed a strand of hair out of her eyes. "I know you've enjoyed your freedom while you've been here, but Tess misses you. It's no fun when your best friend won't play with you anymore."

"I'm not her best friend," Abby protested. "Miki Nakama is."

Gran looked Abby in the eye. The ache in Abby's stomach worsened. Deep down, she knew Tess didn't follow her around because she was trying to bug her. She did it because she liked being with her.

"I've got something for you." Gran stood up and pulled some money out of her pocket. "This is yours. It's for helping me at the market today. I wanted to give it to you now so Tess wouldn't feel left out."

"Thanks." Abby glanced at the bills, then shoved them in her pocket.

"You earned it," Gran said. Abby had the feeling Gran was going to say something more, but she only picked up the pail of milk and turned to the door.

Suddenly the barn filled with shrill, insistent barking.

"Woof!" Tess raced toward them. "WOOF, WOOF!"

"What's wrong?" cried Gran.

"Treasure," panted Tess. "Wonderful, wonderful treasure!"

Abby groaned. "Not again."

Tess ignored her and tugged on Gran's arm. Milk sloshed over the top of the pail. "Come and see! I was digging in the straw and there it was!"

Gran set the pail down and let herself be pulled along. "Okay, okay," she laughed. "I'm coming."

Abby's mouth fell open as she neared the big pile of straw near the barn door. There, right in the middle of the pile, was a toothbrush. Even though the handle was dented and half the bristles were missing, she could tell it was hers. Beside the toothbrush was a bent spool and a tangle of silver ribbon.

"I don't understand," she said.

"The kid did it," said Tess. She pulled out her imaginary notebook and flipped through the pages. "It's all in here. I've been spying on her."

Abby blinked. "But . . ."

"Boo Boo and I saw her take the silver ribbon," continued Tess. She smiled and hugged her monkey to her chest. "We searched the whole farm, but couldn't find it. We knew she hid it somewhere. Just like buried treasure. Now we've found it!"

"Come on," snorted Abby. "You expect me to believe the kid snuck into the bathroom, stole my toothbrush and hid it in the barn? What about all the other missing things? Gran's gardening glove and my sparkle pen and my letter. And I'm still missing a sock, by the way. It doesn't make any sense."

"You think I took them?" cried Tess.

Gran held up her hands. "Nobody is accusing you, Tess. You know, Abby, smart goats have been known to unlatch gates. That might explain how the kid gets out of the corral so often."

"But my toothbrush was in the house," protested Abby. "Goats can't turn doorknobs. It's impossible!"

Tess crossed her arms over her chest. "It wasn't me."

"We'll figure it out," Gran said. "But first we'd better make sure there's nothing else hidden in this barn."

Abby picked up her toothbrush and grimaced. It certainly looked like an animal had been gnawing on it.

Gran and Abby and Tess searched through the straw, then took a quick look around the rest of the barn. Abby found her sparkle pen next to a bag of grain. Tess spotted a single chewed finger from Gran's gardening glove near the barn entrance. There was no sign of Abby's letter to Dirk.

When the hunt was over they headed for the house. Abby strode on ahead so she wouldn't have to listen to Tess's chatter. There was no way the kid could be responsible for this. It was absurd! Abby flung open the farmhouse door, then stopped in her tracks.

Standing in the middle of the kitchen, with a broken cookie jar at its feet, was the kid.

15 Case Closed

"Baaah."

The kid glanced at Abby, then bent its head to nibble one of the chocolate chip cookies that were scattered across the floor.

"See," cried Tess, skipping into the kitchen. "I told you!"

Abby stared. "How did she get in here? The door was shut. I saw it with my own eyes."

"Maybe it wasn't shut all the way," suggested Gran. "You know how hard it is to close. I've been meaning to get it fixed."

"I was right," Tess giggled. "She's a goat burglar."

Abby shook her head in disbelief. "Sure, she knows how to get into my pockets for treats. But opening doors? That's crazy."

"There's only one way to find out," Gran said. She set the milk pail on the counter and shooed the goat outside. Shutting the door firmly, she turned to Abby. "Call her."

Feeling a bit foolish, Abby yelled, "Mocha-Clover-Bambi-Cinnamon-Nutmeg-Dandelion. Come here, girl." She looked at Gran and shrugged. "I still can't decide on a name."

They waited. At first nothing happened, then they heard a soft thump. Then another and another and the kitchen door popped open. The kid trotted straight to Abby and stuck its nose in her pocket.

Tess pulled out her invisible notebook and scribbled furiously. She pretended to slam it shut, then grinned. "Case closed."

Abby felt dazed as she and Gran led the kid back to the barn. "I still can't believe she took all that stuff," she said, watching Gran secure the corral gate with baling twine. "Why would she do that? Haven't I been feeding her enough?"

Gran shook her head. "That's not it. Some people say goats will eat anything, but it's not true. The most unusual thing I've known them to eat is paper."

"Paper?" Abby thought of her missing letter and groaned. Dirk would laugh when he heard it

had been a tasty snack for a goat.

"Goats are extremely curious creatures," Gran explained. "Like lots of animals, they're attracted to things that are shiny or scented. Maybe the kid got bored and decided to have some fun. Who knows?"

"You're going to need better latches," Abby said. "Goat-proof ones."

Gran linked arms with Abby and they walked back to the farmhouse. "Well, at least I don't feel like I'm losing my mind anymore. Thanks to Tess."

Abby chewed on her lip. If she hadn't made Tess feel so unwanted, she'd have told Abby that she suspected the kid of stealing things. They could have solved the mystery together. And Abby could have saved herself a lot of worry.

The lousy feeling in the pit of her stomach returned. It stayed with her while she ate supper and got ready for bed. It was a relief to snuggle under the covers with her diary and let the words flow. She wrote about Tess's secret hideout and the missing objects. And how she'd suspected

Gran was getting too forgetful to live on the farm alone, when all along it had been a mischievous goat. She wrote for an hour. When she finally laid her head on the pillow and closed her eyes, she felt a hundred times better.

The next morning Abby, Tess and Gran went back to the Farmers' Market. Abby worked just as hard as she did yesterday, but today she had something special in mind. She caught Gran watching her a few times, but she just smiled and sold more soap. The hours passed quickly and nobody noticed when Abby slipped away from the booth just before closing.

"Sorry I'm late," she said, hopping into the truck ten minutes later. She was out of breath from running. "I had an errand to do."

Gran raised one eyebrow but didn't say anything. She started the truck and they headed down the road.

Halfway home Abby took a deep breath and turned to her sister.

"Listen, Tess." As she spoke, the ache in her stomach eased a bit. "I didn't mean to get so crazy this week. It's just that I've never had my own room before. I shouldn't have barged into your secret hideout. I'm sorry."

Tess didn't speak for a moment. She fiddled with the strap of her bathing suit and Abby had the sinking feeling that an apology wouldn't be enough this time. Then Tess looked up. "That's okay," she said with a smile.

Gran drove up the driveway and parked the truck. But Abby didn't reach for the door handle. Instead, she pulled something out from under her shirt.

"Here, Tess," she said. "This is for you."

Tess eagerly ripped the paper off the square package. She paused, then sniffed the object. "A notebook?"

"A diary, actually." Abby flipped it open and showed Tess the blank pages. "Mine is really important to me. It's where I keep my private thoughts. I thought maybe you'd like one too, especially since your imaginary one is full."

"My very own diary?"

"A super-secret diary," Abby added with a smile.

Tess threw her arms around Abby's neck.

"I love it."

Abby caught Gran grinning at the two of them. "I bought it at the market with the money I earned yesterday."

"Why don't you show it to your parents," suggested Gran.

Abby had been so intent on giving Tess the diary she hadn't noticed the car parked behind the apple tree. Mom and Dad sat at the picnic table with a pitcher of lemonade between them.

"Mom, Dad," Tess raced across the grass. "Look what Abby gave me!"

"Whoa." Dad laughed as she flew up the porch steps and into his arms. "Aren't you even going to say hello?"

"Hello and look at my diary," Tess said all in one breath. "It's for my top secret stuff. Nobody is allowed to read it. Never, never, never! Except I'll need help with the writing part. You'll help me, won't you Abby?"

Abby grinned and shrugged. "Sure."

"Speaking of secrets," began Mom.

"I dug lots of holes," Tess interrupted,

jumping up and down. "I found gold nuggets and a dinosaur bone and a goat burglar treasure! And I made a secret hideout and learned how to be a spy. Only Abby said I shouldn't ear-drop because it's rude."

"Eavesdrop," corrected Abby. She smiled at her parents. "It's been an interesting week."

"Sounds like it," said Dad, looking a little puzzled. "Actually, we've got some news of our own . . ."

"But Abby never found a name for the baby goat," Tess said, frowning. "I guess it's too late now."

"No it's not," said Abby. The name she'd been searching for had been right under her nose the whole time. "Her name is Missy. Short for Mischief."

Gran burst into laughter. "It's perfect."

"I hate to leave her, though," Abby said. "Babies are so much fun, even though they're a lot of work."

Mom and Dad exchanged glances. "Well, if you liked taking care of a baby goat, then you'll love our news," said Dad, "if you'll ever let us tell you what it is."

"News?" said Abby and Tess at the same time.

Mom patted the bench beside her. "Sit down for a minute, girls."

Abby searched Mom's face. "You still look kind of tired. Maybe we should stay another week."

Mom smiled and pulled Tess onto her lap. "I'm sure Gran would love that, but it's time to come home. And yes, I'm still tired, but there's a reason for it. A wonderful reason."

Abby wrapped her arms around her mother and she leaned her head on her shoulder.

Mom took a deep breath. "We're going to have a baby."

There was silence for a moment. Then everyone tried to speak at once.

"A real live baby?" cried Abby.

"Oh, my word," exclaimed Gran. "What wonderful news!"

"A baby! A baby! We're gonna have a

baby," chanted Tess. She scrambled onto the picnic table and started to dance.

"Not right away," cautioned Dad, catching Tess by one arm. He swung her back down to the porch. "It's not due until after Christmas. That's a long time from now."

Abby put her hand on Mom's belly. A baby. Someone to love and take care of and teach things to. Just like a pet, only better.

"Sometimes the best secrets are the ones you can share with people you love," said Gran, blinking back tears.

Abby hugged Mom and smiled. She couldn't have said it better herself.